All The Better To See You With!

Margaret Wild

Illustrated by Pat Reynolds

A LITTLE ARK BOOK

ALLEN & UNWIN

Kate has four brothers and sisters. They are big and noisy and feisty, even the baby.

Kate is small and quiet and 'no trouble at all', her mother always says with a thankful smile.

It's easy not to take much notice of Kate. Sometimes her family even forgets she's there.

But now and again, when Dad is looking after the other children, Mum makes a special fuss of Kate. She washes her long, brown hair, and blows it dry. Then she brushes it one hundred times to make it shine.

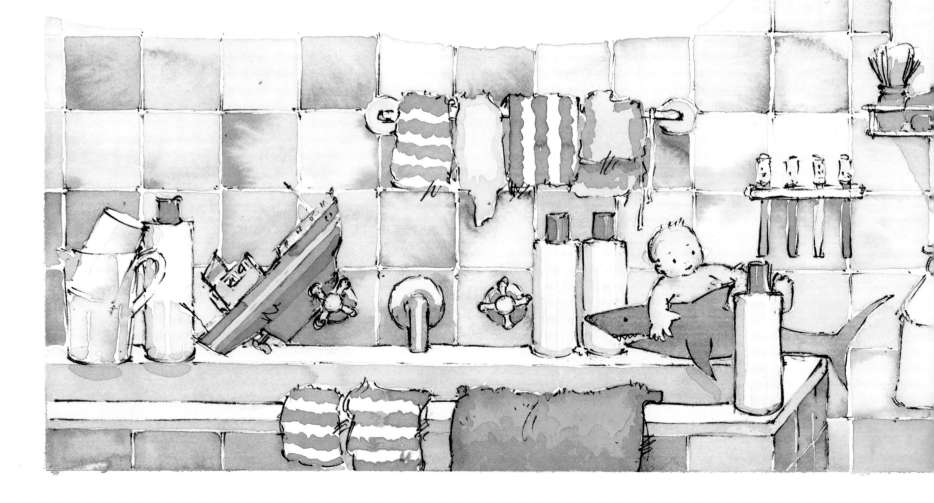

And all the while, she and Kate play the game they've been playing since Kate was a baby.

'What big, white teeth you have!' says Mum.

'All the better to nibble you with, my dear,' says Kate.

'What a big, smiley mouth you have!' says Mum.

'All the better to kiss you with, my dear,' says Kate.

'What big, brown eyes you have!' says Mum.

'All the better to see you with, my dear,' says Kate.

But, although Kate doesn't know it, she really can't see very well at all. When she's sitting close to Mum, she can see the little bump on her nose and the funny freckle on her cheek.

But when Mum's walking home from the bus-stop, all Kate can see is a splash of red, a splash of blue and a splash of brown. She knows it's Mum, because those are her clothes, but her face is just a blurry blob.

Kate is used to blurry blobs and splashes of colour.

When she's in the city, this is what she sees:

When she's in the country, this is what she sees:

When she's at the top of the slippery dip, this is what she sees:

And when she stares out of her bedroom window, this is what she sees:

If Kate were big and noisy and feisty, perhaps someone would say, 'Hey, Kate, why are you sitting so close to the TV?' Or, 'Hey, Kate, why didn't you wave back to Mrs Battiwalla?' Or, 'Hey, Kate, why do you always fall asleep at the movies?'

But Kate is small and quiet and no trouble at all. She doesn't know what other people can see, and no-one thinks to ask her what she sees.

One Sunday, at the beach, while the other children are making sandcastles, Kate goes off on her own to paddle. When she comes out of the water, she can't see her family anywhere.

She runs up and down the beach, peering this way
and that.

At last, her mother catches her by the arm, takes her
back to the umbrella, and wraps a towel around her.

'What was the matter?' Mum asks. 'You ran right past
us twice.'

Kate shivers. 'I couldn't see you. All the umbrellas and
the people look the same.'

'What?' says her mother. Then she says very carefully,
'Can you see the ship over there, Kate, on the horizon?'
'What ship?' says Kate. 'What horizon?'

Dad says slowly, as if he's thinking, 'Can you see the
seagulls over there, Kate, on the pier?'
'What seagulls?' says Kate. 'What pier?'

Mum and Dad stare across the sand at their noisy, feisty family. Then they put their arms around Kate.

'My little Kate,' says Mum. 'I'm so very sorry.'

'We should have noticed ages ago that you can't see properly,' says Dad. 'You must be short-sighted. That means you can't see faraway things clearly. You need spectacles, my girl. Glasses.'

'Glasses!' says Kate. 'For me?' and she feels a flutter of excitement in her stomach.

So, Mum makes an appointment, and takes Kate to the eye-specialist to have her eyes tested.

Then Kate chooses the frames she likes.

'They make you look older,' says Mum, 'and very important.'

Kate has to wait a week for her glasses to be made. It's a long, long week.

'You're lucky,' says her sister. 'I wish I was getting spectacles.'

'Speck, speck, speck!' shouts the baby, climbing on Kate's knee.

She hugs him, her eyes shining, and thinks, 'Soon I'll be able to see, really see! What will it be like?'

A week later, Kate puts her new glasses on her nose.
Her heart thumps. She shuts her eyes, then opens them.

Now, when Kate's in the city, this is what she sees:

When she's in the country, this is what she sees:

When she's at the top of the slippery
dip, this is what she sees:

And when she stares out of her
bedroom window, this is what she sees:

And now and again, when Mum brushes her hair and says, 'What big, shining spectacles you have!' Kate laughs and says, 'All the better to see you and Dad and the kids and the baby and *everything* with, my dear!'